FIRST AMERICAN EDITION

First published in Great Britain
by Walker Books Ltd., London

Library of Congress Cataloging-in-Publication Data
Hayes, Sarah.
Bad egg.
Summary: A prose elaboration on Humpty Dumpty's
experience on the wall, based on the familiar
nursery rhyme.
[1. Folklore.   2. Nursery rhymes – Adaptations]
I. Voake, Charlotte, ill.   II. Title.
PZ8. 1. H324Bad   1987   [398.2] [E]   87-2648

PRINTED IN ITALY

BAD EGG
THE TRUE STORY OF HUMPTY DUMPTY

Written by
Sarah Hayes

Illustrated by
Charlotte Voake

JOY STREET BOOKS
Little, Brown and Company
Boston   Toronto

Humpty Dumpty sat on a wall.
A horse came up to watch.
"Can you sit on this wall, horse?"
said Humpty Dumpty.

"Of course," said the horse.
And he did.

Then he wobbled and wobbled,
and then he fell off.

Humpty Dumpty laughed.
"Tee hee," he said,
"you've hurt your knee."

Humpty Dumpty sat on the wall.
Another horse came up to watch.
"Can you stand on this wall, horse?"
said Humpty Dumpty.

"Of course," said the horse.

And he did.

Then he wobbled and wobbled,
and then he fell off.

Humpty Dumpty laughed.
"Oh dear," he said,
"you've hurt your ear."

Humpty Dumpty sat on the wall.
A man came up to watch.
"Can you stand on one leg
on this wall, man?"
Humpty Dumpty said.

"Yes," said the man, "I can."

And he did.

Then he wobbled and wobbled,
and then he fell off.

Humpty Dumpty laughed.
"Ho ho," he said,
"you've hurt your toe."

Humpty Dumpty sat on the wall.
Another man came up to watch.
"Can you stand on one leg
and juggle with bricks
on this wall, man?"
Humpty Dumpty said.

"Well," said the man,
"I think I can."
   And he did.

Then he wobbled and wobbled,
and then he fell off.

Humpty Dumpty laughed.
"Go to bed," he said,
"you've hurt your head."

Humpty Dumpty sat on the wall.
The King came up to watch.
He saw his horses
and he saw his men.

And the King was terribly, terribly cross.

"Come down," the King said.
"Come down from that wall."
But Humpty Dumpty said nothing at all.
He stood on one leg and juggled with bricks.
He did cartwheels and headstands
and all sorts of tricks.

Then he wobbled and wobbled,
and then he fell off.
CRASH!

And all the King's horses,

and all the King's men...

put Humpty Dumpty together again.
Said Humpty Dumpty, "After such a great fall,
I'll never ever climb back on that wall."

But he did!

398.2
HAY   Hayes, Sarah

          Bad egg

DATE DUE			25274
	BRODART	03/90	12.95

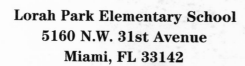

Lorah Park Elementary School
5160 N.W. 31st Avenue
Miami, FL 33142